Copyright © 2012 by NordSüd Verlag AG, CH-8005 Zürich, Switzerland.
First published in Switzerland under the title *Lisas Mohnblume*.
English translation copyright © 2012 by North-South Books Inc., New York 10017.

First published in the United States, Great Britain, Canada, Australia, and New Zealand in 2012
by North-South Books, Inc., an imprint of NordSüd Verlag AG, CH-8005 Zürich, Switzerland.

Translated by David Henry Wilson.
Designed by Elynn Cohen.
Distributed in the United States by North-South Books Inc., New York 10017.
Library of Congress Cataloging-in-Publication Data is available.
ISBN: 978-0-7358-4057-7 (trade edition)
1 3 5 7 9 · 10 8 6 4 2
Printed in Germany by Grafisches Centrum Cuno GmbH & Co. KG, 39240 Calbe, November 2011.

www.northsouth.com
Meet Marcus Pfister at www.marcuspfister.ch.

Marcus Pfister

Ava's Poppy

NorthSouth
New York / London

Every morning Ava crossed the field
in front of her house.

One day she found a poppy.
"You're very beautiful," said Ava.
"Please, can I be your friend?"

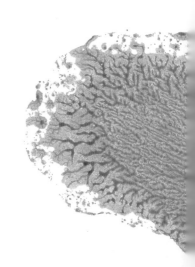

Ava visited her flower every day.
And every day she found it right
away. It stood out in the field, a
lovely shining red. Its petals were
very soft, and sometimes they
moved gently in the breeze.

Together, Ava and her poppy
would look up at the sky.

Ava was always there for her friend.
She protected it from the cold wind.

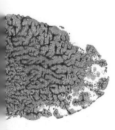

She gave it water when the earth was dry.

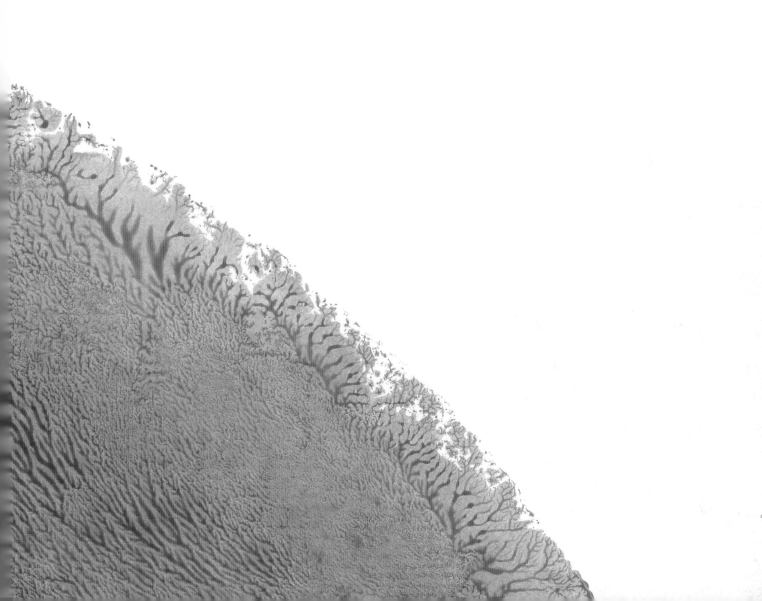

And she put up her umbrella
when it rained too hard.

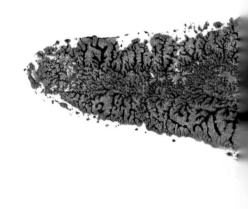

Ava looked after her friend with tender loving care. But then the flower began to lose its petals.

Ava was sad.

Only the round capsule was still
shining fresh and green.

But soon that too became brown and dry.
Ava dug a hole, laid the capsule inside, and
covered it with earth.

"Good-bye, dear poppy," whispered Ava.

Ava made a circle of stones to remind her where the flower once stood.

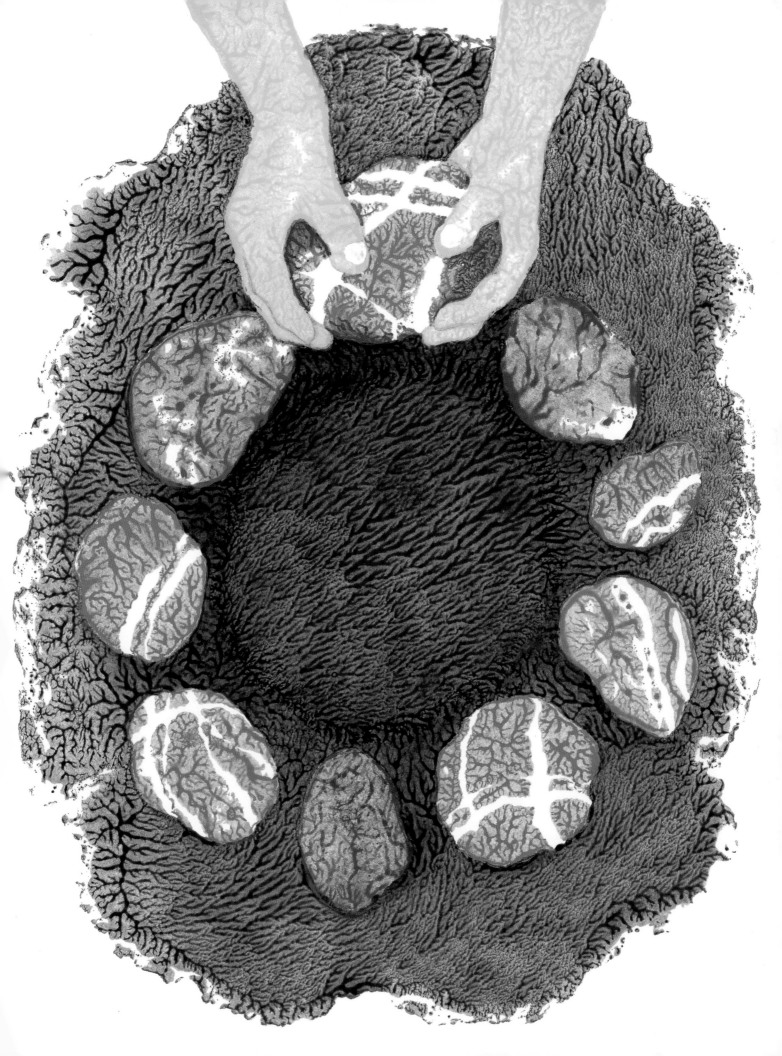

Then winter came.

Ava often thought of her friend. "The snow would certainly have been too cold for my flower," she said to herself.

In the spring, Ava went back to her stone circle. And there she made a wonderful discovery!

In the center of the circle, a tender little plant was reaching up toward the sky.